WHAT'S IN THE DARK?

Parents' Magazine Press/New York

WHAT'S IN THE DARK

BY CARL MEMLING

Pictures by JOHN E. JOHNSON

✳

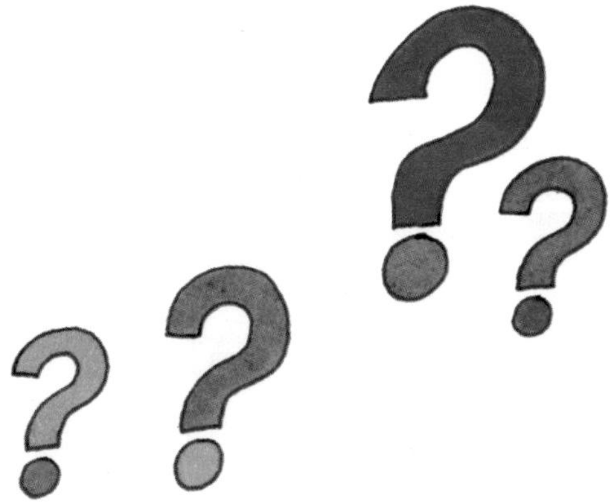

What's in the dark?

After they've clicked the light off
And everybody's said goodnight,
What's in the dark?

The pants you wore today,
Your shoes, your socks, your T-shirt—
They're in the dark.

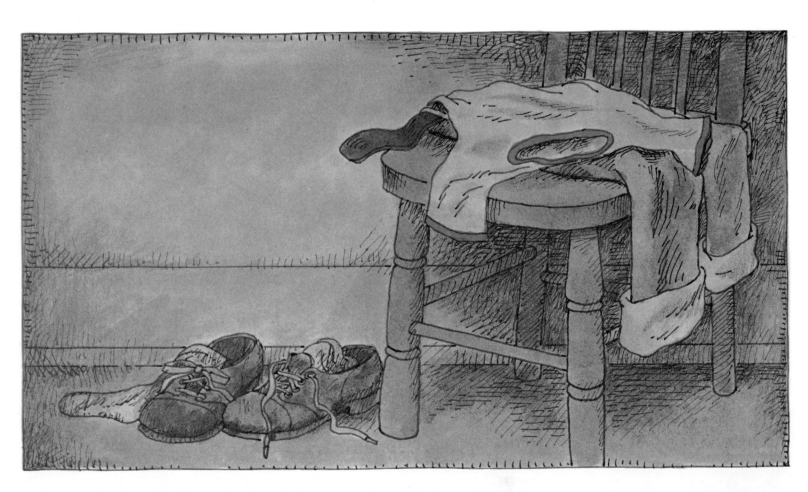

Your crayons in a jumbled pile,
The new ones, used ones, broken ones—
They're in the dark.

The radiator under the window
Makes a jiggety shadow
On the wall
In the dark.

Your cat on the window sill,
Curled in a soft fur ball—
She's in the dark.

Your big sister's record player—
Is it playing   In the dark?

No. Her record player is quiet.
Even the TV in the living room is quiet   In the dark.

Shhhh...
Only the wind whispers outside the window.
Shirts on the clothesline
Swing sleepily
In the wind
In the dark.

The moon in the sky rides slowly
In the dark.

The houses stand with shades drawn,
Like closed eyes in the dark.

Birds sleep,
Squirrels sleep—
All in the dark.

The swings in the park are empty
In the dark.
Nobody slides down the slide
In the dark.

But on the street outside the park,
A policeman walks slowly,
A tall policeman,
Making sure that everything's all right
In the dark.

And on the next street,
On a chair tipped back against the wall,
A fireman sits by the firehouse.
He sits listening for the fire bell.
He'll make sure that everything's all right
If there is a fire in the dark.

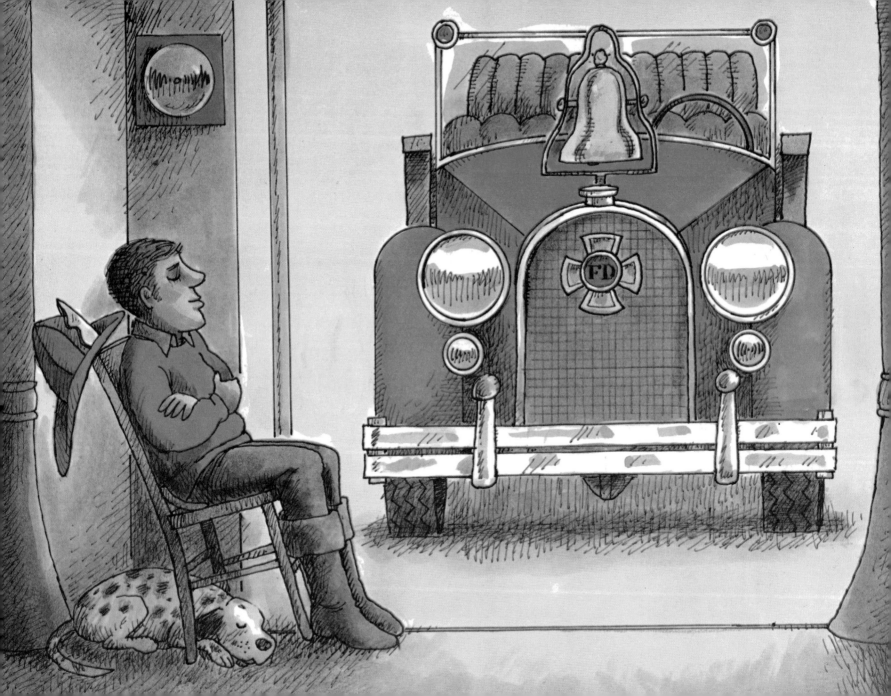

Traffic lights
Flash through the dark.
Red, green,
Red, green—
All night long.

And on the highway,
Whisshh, come the big trucks,
The big trucks bringing food to the city
All night long
In the dark.

An airplane,
High in the dark sky,
Makes a long,
Drawn-out,
Faraway
Sound.

A cleaning truck comes slowly down the street,
Spraying water and slowly sweeping.
Swisssshhhh, go the big round brushes.
Swisssshhhh, swisssshhhh
In the dark.

Shhhh…
Big sister is sleeping.

Mama is sleeping,
Daddy is sleeping—
In their room in the dark.

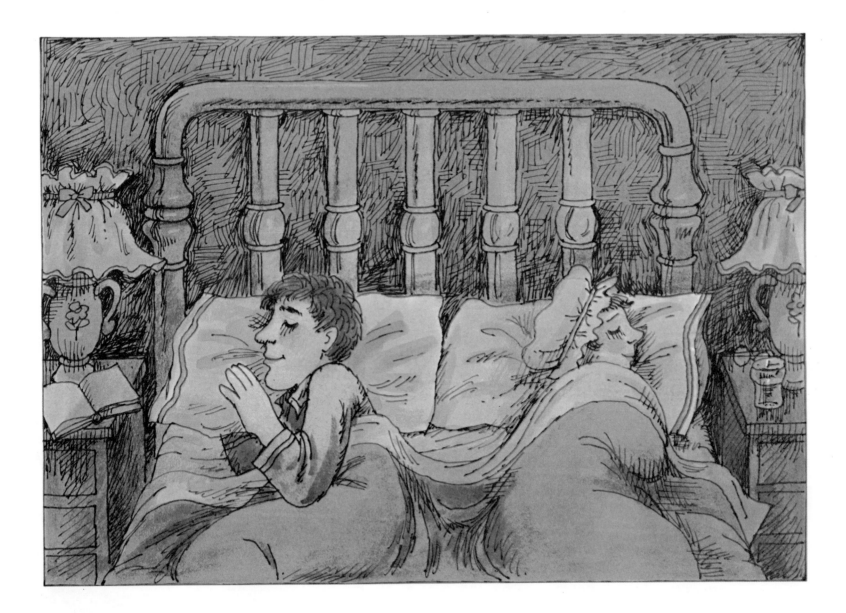

And you, too,
In your bed,
Lying in your soft, warm blanket—
You sleep, too—
Shhh…Shhh…
In the dark.